www.mascotbooks.com

Football Freddie & Fumble the Dog: Gameday in Atlanta

For more information, please contact:
Mascot Books
620 Herndon Parkway #320
Herndon, VA 20170
info@mascotbooks.com

Library of Congress Control Number: 2018910324

CPSIA Code: PRT1018A
ISBN-13: 978-1-64307-204-3

Printed in the United States of America

FOOTBALL FREDDIE
& FUMBLE THE DOG
Gameday in Atlanta

#3

Marnie Schneider
Jonathan Witten

Illustrated by
D. Moore

*Dedicated to Falcons
fans everywhere.*

Rise Up!

Hi! My name's Freddie, and this is my trusty companion Fumble. We're on our way to the football stadium in Atlanta to see the home team play today!

My friend Gabe has been waiting for us to arrive here at Tybee Island. His bulldog Gridiron is here too! Gridiron got his name because he loves watching football, just like me! Even though he looks tough, he's really very gentle, just like Gabe. Look Fumble, he's brought you a matching bowtie to show off your team pride! How thoughtful!

Here at **Tybee Island** you can see the Tybee Lighthouse in the distance. There's been a lighthouse here since 1736.

"Gridiron" is a nickname for a football field.

Georgia's state motto is "Wisdom, Justice, Moderation."

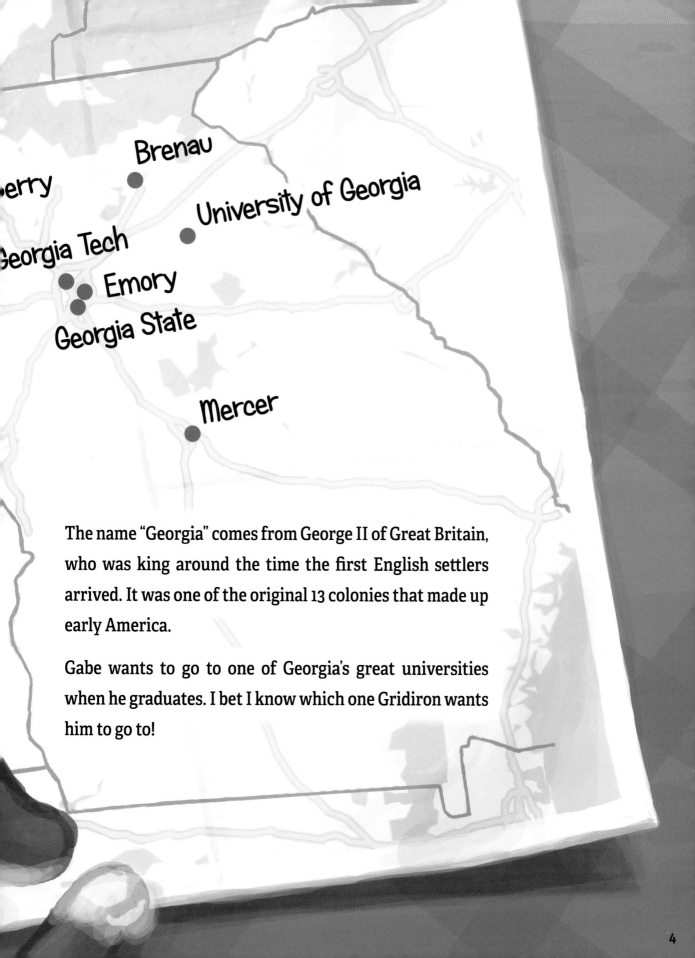

erry

Brenau

University of Georgia

Georgia Tech

Emory

Georgia State

Mercer

The name "Georgia" comes from George II of Great Britain, who was king around the time the first English settlers arrived. It was one of the original 13 colonies that made up early America.

Gabe wants to go to one of Georgia's great universities when he graduates. I bet I know which one Gridiron wants him to go to!

Savannah is the oldest city in Georgia.

GHOSTBUSTING BY RAY PARKER

Let's start our journey here in Savannah's Historic District! Look at these beautiful old houses and city streets, Fumble. They're the same as when they were built back in 1733.

In these old historic houses, you can almost believe all those ghost stories. Gabe says not to worry. He and Gridiron will protect us!

Down to the south near the border with Florida is the Okefenokee Swamp! Say that three times fast! The name means "The Land of the Trembling Earth."

Let's hop on a boat and take a tour down these old waterways. Be sure to put on your life preserver, everyone! Yikes! An alligator just splashed our boat with his tail. Thanks for letting me use your handkerchief to dry off, Gabe!

Okefenokee Swamp was designated a National Natural Landmark in 1974.

Not too far away is the **National Infantry Museum**! Gabe wanted to come here in order to learn more about the history of these heroic men and women and honor their memories. It's important to remember those who served and are currently serving to protect us. I'm glad Gabe thought to come here!

Stone Mountain is 1,686 feet tall at the top.

Here's another one of Georgia's Natural Wonders—Stone Mountain! Gabe says there's a cable car that can take us up to the top. Don't look down, Fumble!

A green jacket is awarded to the winner of the Masters each year.

Before we head on to Atlanta, Gabe and Gridiron want to stop by **Augusta**. This is where the Masters, one of the four major golf championships in the U.S., is held every year! This is the famous Hogan Bridge, which will take us over the creek to the 12th hole. That jacket looks pretty great on you, Fumble!

Time to head on into Atlanta, the capital of Georgia. Our first stop is the **Fox Theater**. Gabe and Gridiron say they love coming here to watch movies, theater plays, and concerts because it's so accessible for Gabe! Georgia is known for being home to many great musicians. Did you know that Gridiron's favorite band is the B-52s?

The Georgia Aquarium is the only place in the world you can swim with whale sharks.

Our next stop is the **Georgia Aquarium**. When it was opened in 2005, it was the largest aquarium in the world!

My favorite exhibit is the sea lions, but Gabe loves the jellyfish. Just don't try to eat them with your peanut butter, Fumble!

The control tower at Atlanta's airport is the tallest in the U.S. at 398 feet. That's as tall as 1.3 football fields!

Centennial Olympic Park was the site of the 1996 Summer Olympics, though these days you don't need to be an Olympian to visit. Phew! I've worked up quite a sweat from walking around today. Gabe recommends we check out the Fountain of Rings—it's got 251 water jets that are a great way to cool off. Gabe is a wonderful tour guide!

It's getting awfully late in the day, but Gabe won't let us head off to the game without first stopping by the Martin Luther King, Jr. Historical Park. Let's go see the church where he was a pastor, his boyhood home, and also pay our respects at his gravesite.

RY OF THE CIVIL RIGHTS

REV. MARTIN LUTHER KING
1929 ~ 1968
"Free at last, Free at las
Thank God Almighty
I'm Free at last."

CORETTA SCOTT KING
1927 — 2006
"...nd now abide Faith, Hope,
...ove, These Three; but the
...reatest of these is Love."
1 Cor. 13:13

Among his
other achievements,
Martin Luther King,
Jr. received the Nobel
Peace Prize
in 1964.

The world's largest peach cobbler is made every year in Georgia for the Georgia Peach Festival.

Looks like we arrived at the stadium just in time to catch some of the tailgating action! Fumble is drooling at all the peach cobbler. I think I'll try some biscuits and gravy first, while Gabe's going right for some fried okra!

Afterward, Gabe volunteers to get Georgia peaches for everyone. They're so delicious, it's no wonder they're one of the most notable symbols of the state of Georgia! Gabe is so considerate!

There's really nothing like the feeling in the stadium right before a football game! They put a lot of thought into making it accessible for everyone. Let's find our seats before the **National Anthem** starts. Gabe knows to take off his hat to show respect.

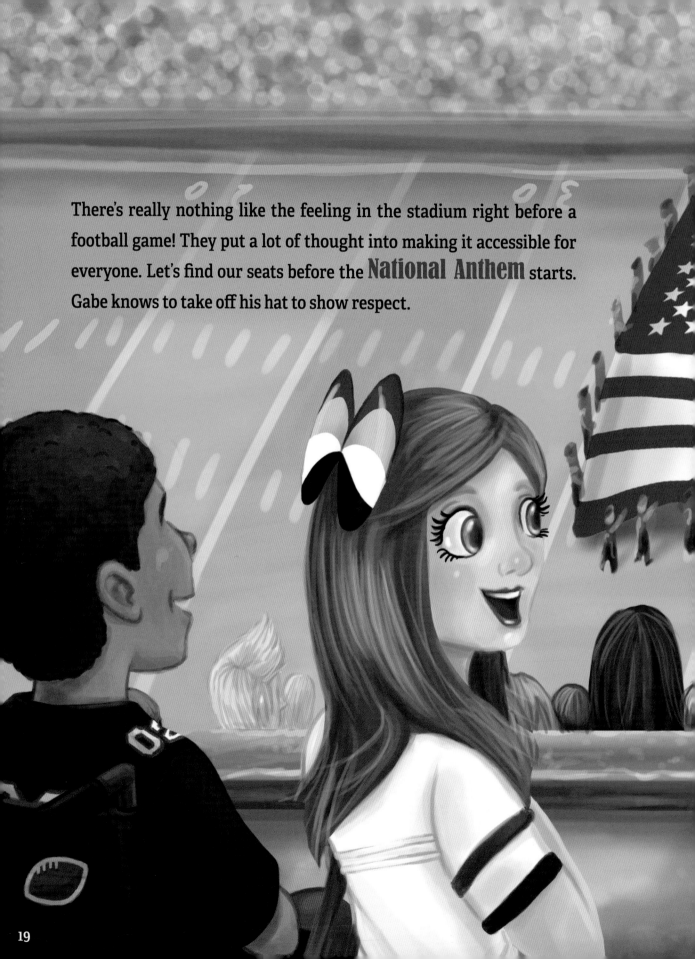

The home team's colors are red, black, white, and silver.

The game has started! It looks like the Falcons are trying to run the football. Their runner has broken free of a tackle and is still going! He's made it all the way to the **endzone**! That's six points for the Falcons!

The team on offense can either run, kick, or throw the football.

Look out! One of the players has dropped the ball. Oh no, the other team has picked it up and run it to their endzone for a touchdown. Gabe can't bear to see what's happening!

Both of the teams are going into the locker room to refocus and get ready for the second half of the game, which means that it's time for the **halftime** show. Gabe explains that the police officers, first responders, and members of the military are helping retire one of the jersey numbers of a former player. What an honor!

RISE UP!

Our cheering worked! This time, it was the other team who fumbled the football and our team who scored. Gabe reminds us that we need to be respectful to everyone, even the other team.

What a day, Fumble! We've seen so many great sights here in Georgia—
I want to get home as soon as possible to write them all down so I don't
forget anything. Though I need to write Gabe and Gridiron a thank-you
card first! Next weekend is another fantastic football city!

XOXO *(that's football language),*
– Football Freddie and
Fumble the Dog

About the Authors

A Philadelphia native now living in the South, Marnie's life has been driven by sports. Her grandfather, Leonard Tose, was a longtime member of the "club" as the owner of the Philadelphia Eagles. He was also the founder of the Ronald McDonald House and helped build NFL Films. From him, Marnie learned the importance of family, sports, and charity. Her series, *Football Freddie and Fumble the Dog* is her way of giving back to the many great football communities across the nation.

Jonathan Witten is the third generation in a long line of football fans. Diagnosed with neuroblastoma cancer at a young age and unable to walk or talk until age 5, he went on to play varsity football and is currently attending college. He loves watching football with his younger brother and younger sister. His grandmother, Susan T. Spencer, was

Leonard Tose and the young author.

the first woman in pro football to be the vice president, legal counsel, and acting general manager of the Philadelphia Eagles. She's the author of *Briefcase Essentials* and co-author of *Gameday in Philadelphia*, the first book in the Football Freddie series. Susan also runs a very successful nonprofit called A Level Playing Field, which helps kids play sports safely.

Georgia Facts:

State Fruit
Georgia Peach

Flag

Year of Establishment
1788

Nickname
The Peach State, Empire State of the South

State Song
"Georgia on My Mind"